Cinderella lives with her stepmother and stepsisters. There is great excitement one day when the king and queen invite everyone to a grand ball. When the day of the ball arrives and her sisters leave for the palace, Cinderella is left alone at home. But then something very strange happens...

A catalogue record for this book is available from the British Library.

First edition

Published by Ladybird Books Ltd Loughborough Leicestershire UK

Printed in England (7)

DISNEP

CINDERELLA

Ladybird Books

Once upon a time, in a far away place, there lived a beautiful girl called Cinderella. She lived in an old house with her stepmother and two stepsisters.

They were horrid to her because she was beautiful and they were not. Cinderella's only friends were the mice who lived in the house, and Bruno the dog.

Cinderella worked hard in the
house. She wore old clothes and
did all the cleaning, polishing,
cooking and mending.

Her stepsisters, who were very
ugly, dressed in fine clothes and
went out to parties.

One day an invitation came from
the palace. The king and queen
were giving a ball for their son,
the prince.

All the young ladies in the land
were invited to attend. "The prince
will choose his bride at the ball!"
shrieked the ugly sisters.

"How exciting!" said Cinderella,
her eyes sparkling.

But her cruel stepmother and stepsisters laughed at her. "How can *you* go to the ball? You have nothing to wear. And anyway, you will have to help us to get ready," they said.

The day of the ball arrived and the ugly sisters found lots of jobs for Cinderella to do.

"Cinderella, wash my stockings
and curl my hair!" shouted one,
loudly.

"Cinderella, find my fan and fetch
my dancing slippers!" called the
other. And all the time,
Cinderella's stepmother scolded her
for being so slow.

At last the ugly sisters were dressed
in their finest clothes, ready for the
ball. Their coach arrived and they
climbed in, chattering and singing

happily. They waved to their
mother and called, "Goodbye,
Cinderella!" and off they went.

Cinderella went out into the garden
and cried and cried. "If only I
could go to the ball," she sobbed.
Suddenly she saw a strange yellow
light in the sky. Cinderella rubbed

her eyes to see if she was dreaming.

But when she looked again she saw
a lady standing in front of her
holding a wand.

"Don't cry, Cinderella," said the lady, kindly. "I am your fairy godmother. You *are* going to the ball. But first, you must fetch me a large pumpkin."

Cinderella found the biggest and fattest pumpkin in the garden and Bruno and the mice helped her to bring it to the fairy godmother.

With a wave of her wand and a flash of light, the fairy godmother turned the pumpkin into a beautiful coach. Cinderella could not believe her eyes!

Waving her wand again, the fairy godmother turned the mice into fine horses and a driver for the sparkling coach.

And Bruno the dog became a very handsome footman. "There," said the fairy godmother. "Now you are ready!"

But then she saw that Cinderella was still wearing her old dress. "Oh, dear me!" said the fairy godmother. "That will never do!"

She waved her magic wand once more. Suddenly Cinderella's old clothes disappeared and she was dressed in the most beautiful ballgown that she had ever seen.

She had dainty glass slippers on her feet and long satin gloves on her hands.

"Oh!" she said. "How can I *ever* thank you."

"Just have a wonderful time," said her fairy godmother. "But remember, the magic stops at midnight." Cinderella promised that she would be home by midnight.

Then she stepped into the magic coach and waved goodbye to her fairy godmother. She *was* going to the ball.

The palace looked splendid. Every room was filled with music and lights.

The court ladies were dressed in their very best clothes and finery but Cinderella was, by far, the most beautiful there.

Everyone wondered who she could be. Even her own stepsisters did not recognise her.

The prince looked at no one else and danced with Cinderella all night. Time passed so quickly that she forgot about the promise to her fairy godmother.

And then Cinderella heard the clock as it began to strike midnight...**one, two, three**...

Without a word Cinderella ran
from the ballroom...**four, five**...
and down the palace steps...**six,
seven**...

She ran so fast that she lost one
of her glass slippers on the steps.
But she had no time to pick it up
...**eight, nine**...

The magic coach was waiting for

her at the bottom of the steps. She
jumped in quickly and the coach
sped away into the night, leaving
the palace far behind...**ten,
eleven**...

As the clock struck twelve, the
magic coach, driver, footman *and*
horses all disappeared. The magic
had stopped.

Next morning, the kingdom was
filled with news of the ball and the
prince's search for the owner of a
glass slipper. The Grand Duke was
visiting every house in the land
with the glass slipper in his hand.

"Don't come back until you have
found the girl who was wearing
this slipper. I will marry only her,"
the prince had said.

Every girl tried on the slipper but it
would not fit any of them.
Cinderella's ugly stepsisters tried
the hardest of all. They pushed and
pulled and tugged and twisted but
still the slipper would not fit.

Just as the Grand Duke was about
to leave the house, Cinderella came
into the room. "Oh!" he said,
turning to her stepmother. "But I
thought you said that there were no
other girls in this house!"

"She's only a servant," said the stepmother. "She did not go to the ball!" And with that she knocked the glass slipper out of the Duke's hand. It fell to the floor with a crash and broke into a hundred pieces.

"Now I will never find the prince's bride," the Duke cried.

Cinderella stepped forward. "Yes, you will," she said, softly. "I have the other slipper." And she pulled it out of her pocket. It slipped easily onto her foot!

The Duke was delighted. His search was over. The ugly sisters and the cruel stepmother were furious that Cinderella should have the other glass slipper. They could not think how it could have happened.

So Cinderella married the prince.
The mice and Bruno the dog went
to live with them in the palace.
And they all lived happily ever
after.